My Name is O

by

Sam Enthoven

To find out more about Sam and his writing, check his homepage –

www.samenthoven.com

First published in 2012 in Great Britain by
Barrington Stoke Ltd
18 Walker Street, Edinburgh, EH3 7LP

www.barringtonstoke.co.uk

ISBN: 978-1-84299-838-0

Printed in China by Leo

Contents

Chapter 1

How to Break into the Bank of England

London. On the roof of Tower 42. 2:16 am.

My name is O. Not zero. It's O like the letter that comes after N in the alphabet. Or what you say when you get a surprise – "oh!"

I am 15 years old, I'm 189 metres above ground level and I'm nervous.

Tower 42 is the fifth tallest skyscraper in London. The twinkling lights of the city spread out below me, as far as I can see. Between the lights are great black shadows where the buildings are. Inside the buildings I imagine the people – eight million humans, most of them asleep.

Do you ever get the feeling that your life isn't your own? Do you ever feel like everything you do, or everything you ever can do, has been chosen for you already? That it was all planned out before you were born, so all you can do is go along with it? Have you felt that way?

I have news for you. *It's true*.

I work for the people who mapped out your life for you. They rule you and they rule me too. They planned my life from the start. I was born in a special breeding programme run by our secret masters, and then trained for years until my skills met their needs. Every second of my life has belonged to them. But that will end tonight – one way or another.

I walk to the edge of the roof, and step off.

The silk above me takes my weight no problem – there's not even a jolt. I swing my legs forward and settle the straps until I sit in mid air.

I'm flying.

Relax. I may not be ... normal, but I'm no superhero. I'm using a paraglider. It's a bit like a para*chute*, but it's open before you jump. Imagine a wing made of silk, 8 metres wide and as black as a shadow. That's all that anyone who happens to look up will see as I pass above them – a shadow in the night.

It takes 4 minutes for the glider to drop me to my target. I have cords in each hand that open flaps in the wings made to act like air brakes. Once or twice I pull these to change course but for the rest of the time I have nothing to do but wait. Between my feet I watch a black taxi head north up Old Broad Street. From up here, it is the size of the nail on my thumb.

I look at my target – a low, grey chunk of a building just two blocks away from me to my south-west. That's where I'm going – the Bank of England.

I've chosen to break in to the Bank through the top of one of the lift shafts. That means that I am on the look-out as I approach for a sort of hut on the roof where the lift gear will

3

be. You find these on the roofs of most big buildings. They have a door so workmen can get in to do repairs. Handy for me.

After 3 minutes and 58 seconds I pull the cords hard to fold the paraglider wing. My feet meet the rooftop and I jog five steps to lose some speed. Then I've landed, making no sound other than a whisper as the black silk of the glider falls behind me. It's perfect. It should be – I did my first parachute jump when I was six. The door I want is right beside me. The lock is so easy to pick I'm almost insulted.

And I'm inside.

Chapter 2
Down

You want to know how to break into any building? I have trained for the last ten years to do just that. But for you I can boil it down to two key things you need to remember. Here's the first:

Everyone is *on a budget*. When they build things, they only have so much time and money to spend. This is the case for the people who built your house and it is just as much the case for the people who built the Bank of England.

So when they built the Bank, they looked for the most likely ways that someone might try to break in and came up with ways to stop them. They did a good job. The Bank's doors and windows are well protected. The walls are very thick, hard to climb and covered with cameras and alarms. It is basically impossible to break in from the ground. But not from the roof – that's where the money ran out. I guess it didn't seem so likely that someone would, say, paraglide onto the Bank roof.

It seems they didn't spend too much on security inside the lift hut either. There is a control box with a lock that is even easier to open than the lock on the door – I open it, pick a button, and press. The motor starts up. The wheels begin to turn. By the time I've safely folded up the glider and hidden it behind the door, the lift cab has arrived.

I'm headed underground, to the deepest, most secret level the Bank of England has. It's a long way down, so I'm not going to take the stairs.

A useful fact about lifts is that every cab has an extra set of controls on its roof as standard. There's another lock for me to pop before I can get to the buttons but I think you may have noticed by now that I'm good with locks.

The button is a "dead man's switch" – a kind you have to press and hold. I press and down I go, riding on the roof.

I keep well clear of the cables so they don't snag my clothes and rip my limbs off. And I don't look down over the back of the cab, because I know that's where the counter-weight will pass.

The counter-weight is a slab of cold steel that weighs more than a ton. I know to expect it but it still shocks me when it shoots past at something like 60 km an hour. I'm nowhere near it but still I feel the hair move at the back of my head as it passes. I can't help but think about what it would have done to my head if I'd looked down at the wrong moment. I give a small shiver.

The dust on the top of the lift is so thick that it's more like fur. The lift shaft is warm, too, which makes the dirt feel greasy. And it's dark.

I'm sitting on the top of a lift as it sinks into the deepest levels of the Bank of England, with lethal machinery all around me, in total darkness. If I was anyone else, I would be even more nervous now than I was before. But there's a smile on my face. I've never been this happy in my whole life.

My name is O. My parents are called M and K. As you can see, my kind are given letters of the alphabet for our names. We are bred for our ... talents.

Our masters call us the Blanks. We spy, steal, kill – whatever our masters need us to do. Apart from our masters (and now, I guess, you) no one knows we exist.

I have never met my father and I've not seen my mother in ten years. I have no other family, no friends, no belongings and no home – since my fifth birthday I've been moved again and again, without warning, from place to place, from teacher to teacher as I learned my skills.

We are trained to have no identity – to be nothing, a void. I had very little rest time and if my teachers found that I had used it to listen to music, or read a book, they beat me. If I ever tried to have anything of my own, so I could point to it and say "this is me", I was punished with pain. I am Blank. We are like clay, for our masters to shape as they wish. That's the lesson I was to learn.

But they failed to teach me it.

Alone, in secret, I learned the hardest skill of all: *to make myself*. I built a personality, a *me*, from whatever scraps I could snatch when no one was looking.

My name is O. Not zero: O. I am *not* nothing. I am fabulous and spectacular. And tonight, at last, is when I get to prove it.

Chapter 3
Being Lara

Thirty floors down the lift stops. The noise of the motor cuts out and everything is still. I pop the lock on the hatch in the roof, open it and drop down onto the floor.

I stand up and at once I notice the lens of a security camera on the wall of the lift. I'm not as worried about that as I might be, for reasons that will soon become clear.

The walls are covered in mirrors. I look at myself.

A young woman stares back at me from the place my own face should be. She is 24 years old, 152 cm tall, with milk-white skin, freckles, a button nose, and crow-black hair cut in a cute but grown-up bob. As I reach out to press the button that will open the lift doors I sneak a look at my eyes in the mirror. They are the colour I need them to be – dark brown, with flecks of pale gold at the rims of each iris. OK – I'm ready.

The doors slide open and I step out into the deepest and most secret level of the Bank of England. I try to move as if I'm not even thinking about it, like I do this walk every day. The lights in the ceiling come on one by one as I pass, filling the room with a soft gold glow.

You may have noticed that the insides of normal banks for the most part look the same. Most banks try to look modern and bright, to make their customers feel safe.

The Bank of England is not like that. The thick, deep, wine-coloured carpet is like velvet under my feet as I walk. My scalp prickles as I imagine the spy cameras tracking my every move from secret spots in the dark oak panels on the walls – the Bank's security systems are the very best in the world. But the Bank's look, its style, is old school. It's all done to remind customers of its fame, its history, its heritage – its *class*.

At the end of the hall is the vault door. I have seen bigger ones, but not many – it must be 3 metres across. I don't know how thick it is, but if I had the right gear I could cut through it, sure. It would only take me … a whole day? Maybe two.

Instead, I walk up to a small panel of oak on the right of the door.

You remember the two key things to keep in mind when you want to get in somewhere designed to keep you out? I'm about to show you the second one.

As I walk up, I trigger a sensor and a wood panel slides back to show a small sheet of plain black glass. It is set into the wall about chest level and it is at an angle so that it is easy to lay your hands on it, which is what I do.

While the system scans my fingerprints and the other marks on my hands, another panel slides open at eye level. I open my eyes wide like a good girl and look into a tiny red light so it can scan them. I know there are cameras watching me still and I hope that it will look as if I knew the eye scanner would be there. In fact I didn't – I only *suspected* it might be. That's why I checked my eyes when I came out of the lift. They should be OK. I guess I'm about to find out.

The black glass plate glows green. When I lift my hands the fingerprints stay on the screen, beside the name of the person the system now thinks I am.

Lara Barber, says the screen. *Personal Account Manager. Secret Question: What is your pet's name?*

The image of a keyboard appears under the glass. A blue cursor flashes on and off as it waits for me to type.

This is no problem. I've made sure I know all about Lara. Of all the security questions I could have been asked this is perhaps the easiest. Lara likes to post photos from her phone on her profile pages on the net – lots of

them are of her cat and she always tags it by
name.

Felix, I type.

INCORRECT, says the screen. *PLEASE
ENTER CORRECT ANSWER, OR FULL SECURITY
LOCKDOWN WILL BEGIN. LOCKDOWN IN 5
SECONDS ... 4 ...*

There's a knot in my stomach, a tingle in
my hands, a prickle of sweat on my fingertips.
If I don't get this right all my plans will come
to nothing. The alarm will go off. The lift will
be locked down. I'll be trapped here, a
prisoner, a failure, a loser.

I swallow back the panic and force myself
to think. I know that Felix is Lara's cat's name
– I've read it at the bottom of something like 30
photos.

3 ... the screen says.

If I was Lara and I had to type her cat's
name as the answer to the security question,
what would I do?

2 ...

The answer comes to me. If I was Lara, I might change the name a little.

1 ...

Fel1x, I type, with a number "1" in place of the letter "i". Then I press the "enter" key, and hope.

The black sheet of glass goes blank. I hear a soft THUNK as heavy bolts slide in their sockets. Then, without a sound, the huge vault door to my left begins to open. I've done it.

The second key thing to remember when you want to get in somewhere designed to keep you out is that every door has a weakness. No matter how strong or thick it is, every door is made to be opened.

For Blanks like me, opening a door is just a case of finding out who it's supposed to be opened by ... and becoming them.

Chapter 4
Blank

The vault door swings closed behind me. Now I can stop being Lara and go back to being me.

I blink, and when I open my eyes they're grey again. My fingers sting as Lara's prints swirl and then vanish from the tips. I reach up high for a huge, fantastic stretch – the discs in my spine make a string of deep popping sounds as I grow back 8 cm in height to my normal 160 cm. Lara is smaller than me. To make myself look like her, I made myself shorter then used the extra mass to look like fat on my

hips and belly. That melts away. Lara's
bobbed hair curls and winds until it's in an
elegant swirl on the front of my head, as dark
a blue as the sky at midnight. Just the way I
like it.

I am Blank. I can change the way I look
just by thinking about it.

I'm a shape-shifter.

This is the talent that our masters bred us
for. This is the reason I've been trained to do
the things I can do. We blend in, copy, take on
the looks of other people to get us any place
our masters need us to be. That's why they
teach us to have no identity of our own. It
makes us better at taking on the identities of
others.

No one knows where the talent comes from
– it's a blip somewhere in our genes, an
accident. I think about that a lot. I think
about how our masters discovered the first of
us. I think of how they still search the world
for more of us to join the ranks.

Because of this secret, this power I have,
my life belongs to my masters. I belonged to

them before I was born, before my parents even met. I never had any chance to do anything, be anything, but what they wanted.

And do you know what the worst thing is? I'm not even good at it.

OK, we Blanks can change our bodies when we choose. We can look how we choose to look, be how we choose to be. But there are some rules we can't get round. We can't change our body mass – if we want to be taller there's less body to go round, so we've got to become thinner. If we want to be shorter, there's extra to use up, so we have to get fatter. That means if you want to be able to become lots of different body shapes and be lots of different people the very worst body shape you can have as your own, the one you start out with every time, is *small and skinny.*

That's me. I'm short, and if I make myself taller I look like a skeleton. It's bad enough to have a talent that takes away your freedom. It's even worse when it's not even that much of a talent to begin with.

But that's enough moaning from me. I've got work to do.

Chapter 5
Stuff

I'm standing in a room full of deposit boxes. Every wall is covered with row upon row of tiny steel doors. Behind each door will be a box containing ... what? There will be jewels, of course – crowns and rings and necklaces too valuable to wear or even display. There will be information, too – papers filled with powerful secrets, kept locked up here like dangerous animals.

They're not what I'm here for, so I walk on past.

After the walls of boxes there's a corridor with doorways on both sides. On the left is a room which seems to have no floor – but then I see that the floor is a pit and the pit is filled with gold coins. For a moment I'm surprised as I know that the Bank's supply of gold bars is kept two levels above me. I would have thought the gold coins would be on the same level, so I stop for a look. That's when I see that these coins are all stamped with the faces of emperors of Ancient Rome.

The pit on my right is filled with rubies. The lamps have green shades and the coloured light makes the stones darker than their normal blood colour – they look like scabs. I keep walking.

The next rooms I pass contain cars. On my left is a pale blue Rolls Royce. On my right is a sports car that looks for all the world like a big red doorstop. It has a badge with an Italian name and a picture of a charging bull. These cars must have been brought down here part by part and carefully put back together, never to be driven.

Have you ever wondered what it is that super-rich people keep in places like this?

Well, now you know – it's stuff. Things they own. Objects so valuable that they can never be taken out and used, sometimes not even looked at. Does owning things like that make any sense to you? It doesn't to me.

There's more of it. On the walls of the next room there is a collection of paintings by Leonardo da Vinci. I recognise the Mona Lisa, so I suppose the one in the museum must be a fake. There are one or two in there that I'll bet no art expert in the world knows even exist.

The room to my right is almost bare, containing only a coffin from Egypt covered in so much gold that it makes King Tut's look plain.

Then, in long glass cases on both walls of the hall, there are weapons.

It starts with guns: a huge collection of everything from modern gold-plated machine guns belonging to African war-lords, to the rifles of the white men that "Won the West" more than 150 years ago. But this collection has murder tools from the whole of history. As I keep walking I leave the guns behind. Now I pass suits of armour and sharp stabbing weapons of all kinds.

I stop for a second at a pair of *wakizashi* – Japanese short swords with shiny black sheaths. OK – I admit that I do feel a little bit tempted by these. But only a little. All I've seen so far are trinkets – *stuff*. I'm here for something far more precious.

At last I reach the end of the long display of riches and weapons. In front of me, reaching from wall to wall and from floor to ceiling, is an enormous mirror.

Chapter 6
Reflection

For a moment I look in the mirror. My hair looks *awesome*.

To Lara Barber, the Personal Account Manager I pretended to be before, the mirror would be the end of the vault. As far as Lara knows, there is nothing behind this pane of glass but walls of steel and concrete and then black London earth. When she stands here she thinks she has seen the Bank's secret heart – seen everything there is to see.

I know better.

The mirror is the clue. For the Bank's real owners – my masters – the mirror is a symbol. It represents the object I've come for. For them, and me, the mirror is like a sign saying "This way, please."

At this moment the question in my mind is *How?*

I stop checking my hair and look at the mirror itself.

The frame is made of black wood, carved into the shape of four giant scorpions. The scorpions face each other – two at the bottom of the mirror, two at the top. They are locked in combat, their claws crossed. Their long tails curl around the mirror's corners until the stingers of the high and low scorpions meet, at the very middle of each of the mirror's sides.

The mirror is a horrible thing. To a normal person, everything about it says *"Don't touch."*

… But my masters are not normal people.

I keep thinking.

Most people are scared of scorpions. And for good reason – scorpions can mean death.

... But my masters do not fear death.

I think I know what to do.

The carved stings of the wooden scorpions stick out from the sides of the frame. If I press my body against the glass and stretch out my arms, the stings are close enough together that I can place my hands on all four at once. So that's what I do.

Two things happen straight away.

First I hear a low electric hum like something has switched on and is powering up. I was right. I've found the secret of the mirror!

Then I feel four sharp pains in my hands – right on the four spots where my skin meets the wooden scorpions. The pains feel like sudden points of strong heat. I pull my hands away. When I look at them I see red spots of blood blossom on the skin.

Tiny holes.

The mirror is moving. The whole wall slides back and lifts into the air to show a secret passage behind. But I stay still. A numb tingle spreads up my arms.

I have been poisoned. Hidden needles must have jabbed out from the mirror when I touched it. A very simple trap. And one I should have expected.

As I've said, every door is meant to be opened by someone. This one is meant to be opened by my masters. It is very unlikely that normal humans like Lara would ever spot the door hidden in the mirror like I've just done – but my masters are careful. They needed to make sure, so they added an extra level of security. Any mortal who presses on the stings to open the door will die.

My vision swims then shrinks, until all I see is a tunnel of darkness. I feel a blow to my knees that seems very far away and it takes a moment to understand that my legs have stopped working and I have dropped to the floor. The path to my goal lies ahead of me. But my heart stutters, then stops, and now it's just a matter of time.

Chapter 7
Flashback

"I have poisoned you," said my mother.

"But ... wh-why?" I was having trouble getting my words out, and not just because of the poison. I was crying too much. It was my fifth birthday.

My mother, M, made a *tutt* noise. "When my father poisoned me I didn't ask why. I asked "What with?"

By now I couldn't speak. My mouth felt like it was frozen and stuffed with cotton wool.

"I have given you Botulin toxin," said M. "It's one of the most powerful poisons on the planet. A dose of just one microgram can kill. I have given you two micrograms."

I couldn't see her, or the table, or the room any more. Everything was dark. But I could still hear her words.

"Your body is shutting down," she explained, sounding bored. "Even now you're not able to breathe. In a minute or two, you're going to die."

There was silence, broken only by grunts and hisses from me.

Then my mother said, "Unless ..."

She must have leaned forward because the next words came from beside my ear.

"Your birth, your life ... those things mean nothing, O – until you prove yourself. From this moment on you must *earn* your right to live. Or don't. It's up to you."

She stood up.

"I'm going to leave you now," she said. "Perhaps one day we'll meet again. But to tell you the truth, O, looking at you now, I doubt it."

The door clicked shut. That was the last time I saw her.

Chapter 8
Poison

Now, as I lie on the floor of the Bank of England's most secret level, I know I must use the last lesson that my mother taught me.

In the ten years since M left, I've spent a lot of time training with poisons. Believe me, it wasn't fun. There were other skills which hurt me as I learned them – combat springs to mind – but poison training is the only one where I had to hurt *myself*. You see, for my kind the secret to fighting poison is simple.

The secret is pain.

There's a numbness that spreads through the body when you're close to death. I can feel it now. It's hard to tell you what it's like, because it's not so much a feeling as the *lack* of a feeling – an emptiness, a nothing, a void. It is death – the end, waiting for you.

Sometimes the numbness comes as a relief. You want to sink into it, let it take you down, because it would be so good to let go of all the pain and suffering.

I can't let myself do that. I have to *face* it.

The pain I feel right now is like a small spark of light in the dark. All around it is the cold, numb blank of death, but the pain is white-hot, searing, scalding. It is what I have to focus on. It is the sign that my body is fighting back, changing, finding a way to survive. The pain is life. I picture myself swimming towards it. The pain gets bigger and bigger, until it is all I can feel.

Now I'm like the sun. I'm like a star, on fire, every atom of me burning up in a huge, screaming, awful agony. But the choice is pain or death. And after what feels like about one million years, it gets easier.

It still feels like my blood has been swapped for boiling acid, like 9,000 volts of electricity are being run through my teeth, like needle-sharp spikes of ice are pushing out of every pore of my skin. But the pain has passed its peak.

I stop shaking and, in a while, I find I can see again.

I'm soaked in sweat. My arms and legs feel like wet paper sacks full of bowling balls. I turn my head.

The fake wall with the scorpion mirror still hangs above me. From where I lie, I can look up and see the dull grey steel behind the glass. It's a good 30 cm thick. It's coming down, starting to close again. I'm going to have to move.

I'm like a broken doll. I do my best to roll under the door but my body is heavy and slow. I only just get through and out of the way before its huge weight hits the floor behind me.

Chapter 9
The Others

I crack my eyes open and start to look around.

I am curled up on a sort of step made of dark green marble, lying on my side. To my right is a corridor. It's very narrow, only about a metre across – not much wider than me. The walls are made of dark stone, with three strange lines cut into them, all the way along on both sides.

On the floor are 26 slabs of black marble, laid out in two rows of 13. Each slab is about 50 cm square, with a letter of the alphabet carved into its centre. The two nearest me say Y and Z; the next ones say W and X, then U and V, and so on. The slabs stretch all along the corridor. When I see the letters on the floor I feel strange, like a finger of ice has touched my spine. At first I don't know why.

On both sides of each carved letter there are small rows of numbers marked on the stone. I read the numbers on Z, from the top left. The first numbers are:

806–842, 894–913, 957–986

The numbers run on like that for three rows and then they stop. The last number looks like this:

2009–

Then I realise they're *dates*. And now the cold feeling has spread to my belly, because I've worked out where I am.

This is a tomb.

This corridor is the grave of the Blanks who have come before me. It's the final resting place of all of them. Everyone who spent their lives in the service of our masters, everyone else who has a letter for a name. The ashes of every single one of them are buried here, under these stones, under this floor.

Stop, I tell myself. I can't think about this now. I've got to get my mind back on the job.

I don't like the look of those strange lines on the walls – this place screams "booby trap". It's time I started to take care. I reach into the two pockets on my belly and my back, and get out the last bits of kit that I brought with me. My gecko pads.

The pads are big, 30 cm across, and I have one for each hand. They'll stick to any surface they can form a seal on, and each one can hold the weight of my whole body for a few seconds. Their handles feel solid and good in my hands. OK. I take my first step out onto the graves.

At the far end of the corridor there is a big round light with a brass frame, above a door. It casts a dim light over the room. Sweat breaks out on the back of my neck and on my palms. I am still in control – my feet still work and I am aware of everything around me. But my mind keeps coming back to the graves under my feet.

As I walk I see that the dates on some of the stones go back much, much further than the ones on Y and Z. Some of the Blanks under these stones died in the 6th Century. That makes my masters nearly 1,500 years old. Why didn't I know that they had ruled us that long? And why – this is the big question for me – why didn't I ever know how many of my kind there have been?

The reason, I realise, is simple. Our masters have kept these things secret from us, just like they keep their existence and my existence a secret from you and your kind. My whole life has been a secret – a secret from you, but also, I start to realise, a secret from myself.

Exactly two and a half metres down the corridor I stop and look down. Just ahead of my right foot is the stone marked P. And on the left … O.

I count the dates. There have been 37 Blanks called O. Even though I've seen the other letter stones the fact still hits me hard. 37 others, just like me. I wonder if they felt the same way I do. I wonder if they thought of the name we share and told themselves, "Not zero. O." I wonder if they felt special and fabulous and important.

And then, at once, I feel very stupid. What am I doing here? Who am I to think I can fight our masters? I am just a letter of the alphabet – one letter in an order that repeats itself over and over. I am a single cog on a tiny wheel of a machine that has run for more than a thousand years.

I'm a fool.

And that's when the trap is sprung.

Chapter 10
Timing

An electric whine comes out of nowhere and makes my heart nearly jump out of my chest. The whine becomes a howl, then a crackle and a SPLAT. The corridor grows light.

In front of me, at the far end, a hard line of white light has formed between the walls, coming from the lowest of the lines cut into the stone. This line of light is at about my knee height and it's coming towards me. As it cuts through the room the air heats up. It's some kind of beam weapon, a laser.

MOVE! I tell my legs. I bend my knees, throw up my hands and jump.

I'm still weak from the poison. The jump is rubbish, but my trusty gecko pads slap the ceiling – and stick. Hanging there, I pull up on my arms and lift my legs just as the spitting beam of hot light sizzles past beneath my feet.

I look back over my shoulder and see the beam reach the end of the corridor. It stops, then comes back again the other way.

The beam is fast. It can go from one end of the corridor to the other in about a second. That's too quick for me to drop to the floor again, or even to lower my legs. Whatever I do next I'll have to do up here.

But just as I'm working this out, things gets worse. I hear another electric whine, another spitting CRACK. A second line of white-hot light forms between the highest wall marks, and I've got *two* beams to deal with.

I'm not safe any more. As long as I hang here, the second beam is about level with my arms.

This is going to be hard.

I move fast. One press of the button on my right gecko pad and I find myself hanging by only one arm. As the upper beam comes towards me I twist my body, swing my weight forward, and reach out with my right hand. I miss the beam but it passes so close to me that I feel the heat of it like a blow-torch on the inside of my right arm. I slap the pad as far along the ceiling as I can reach. It sticks.

Now both beams are about to pass me at the same time, one below me and one above. I'm still keeping my legs up, out of the way of the lower beam, but for this next moment my arms are *on different sides* of the higher beam. It's so close to me that when it passes over my face I can feel its heat on my eyelids. I press the button on the left gecko pad and pull that arm clear, then swing myself forward like I'm on monkey-bars. I slap the left pad back on the ceiling, as far ahead of the *right* pad as I can reach.

I'm doing OK. The beams have passed me and I've got a second before they come back. Even better, I've now moved about a metre further up the corridor than I was before. I've got about three metres more to go – three or four more monkey-swings should take me to the door at the far end. Of course, that's *if* I can time the swings right, *if* the lasers don't get me, and *if* my poor poisoned body doesn't give up first. It already hurts to keep my legs up – my stomach is agony and my arms are starting to shake. But I can't think about that – the beams are on their way back.

I go for it.

For the next few seconds it looks like it might actually work. I repeat my monkey-swing once, twice, three times. I ignore the pain in my stomach as it strains to keep my legs up. It feels like a knife in my guts.

But then, on the fourth swing, my hand slips. It is so slick with sweat that my fingers lose their grip on my gecko pad. WHAM. I hit the floor on my back.

I flip to my feet.

At first it looks like good news. Not only did I not hit a beam on my way down and get cut in half, but now I've got a head start. The beams are on their way down the corridor, away from me. They have to go all the way down and all the way back again to reach me. That gives me almost two seconds to reach the door.

The door is covered with dark green leather held in place with rows of studs. On the left side there's a small, round handle made of brass. I grab it and twist, and that's where the good news runs out.

The handle doesn't turn. No matter how hard I twist it, it doesn't even move. I search the rest of the door, but there's no sign of a lock or any other way I can open it.

Behind me I hear another electric whine start, followed by a spitting CRACK. When I turn to look I see that the beam from the last line in the walls has powered up at last. Now three lines of light make their way up the corridor towards me. They're already halfway.

There is no hope left now and I find that it's almost as if I can watch from somewhere outside my body as I realise that I am about to be cut in three. I think I won't die right away – I'll hit the ground in pieces and lie there, helpless but alive for every moment until my life bleeds out onto the cold black graves of my kind.

My face heats up as the beams get closer. I press myself back against the hard leather. As my eyes water from the light that will kill me I give the brass handle beside me a last, useless twist.

I'm so surprised when the door opens, I fall right through it.

Chapter 11
True Faces

The door clicks shut. I pick myself up –
again – and look around to see where I am
now.

Above and below me there is only black,
except for one light in the centre of the room.
It shines down on the only object in the place
and makes a pool on the floor below. On both
sides the walls are mirrored. The mirrors
show reflection after reflection of me and the
object I have come for. The reflections stretch
on and on, forever.

I've reached my target. This is it.

The object has a frame made of old dark wood, with strange shapes carved on it by hand. It is the size I was told to expect – just under 51 cm wide and 102 cm tall. For now the frame looks empty. It looks like a rectangle of space, hanging in the air, kept up by nothing but its own power.

A woman I have seen before walks from the shadows to stand beside it.

"You got here," says my mother. "Well done."

It's been over ten years since I saw her last. She looks just like I remember, except for one thing – she smiles as she looks at me. M never smiled at me before. Her face is warm, almost as if she's pleased to see me.

I take a step back. M's smile widens so I can see her teeth.

"There's no reason to be scared of me, O," she says. "Not any more. Come closer."

I hesitate. But I obey. As I walk towards her something happens – the empty air in the wooden frame begins to change.

A tiny patch of white seems to form at its centre. It's as if the frame is filled by a pane of see-through glass and someone is breathing on it from the other side. But it's not quite like that, because the white is not warm like breath but cold, like ... frost. Tiny flakes and crystals spread out from the centre of the frame. Some clear glass remains. In the end the clear glass forms a grid that divides the mirror into 11 rows of six.

"Watch," says M.

In each of the 66 white spaces on the grid, something happens. In every one of these small frames I start to see shadows, then outlines, then shapes. Now I can see a person in each space on the mirror, all standing with their backs to me.

The ones I see first are dressed in army uniforms. The next ones are dressed in robes, like priests. The last ones have on dark grey suits, like bankers or presidents would wear. As I stand and stare, trying to work out what all of this means, each and every one of the figures turns to look at me.

My blood turns to ice.

Staring out of the frame are what seem to be 66 grinning skulls. But then I see that the people the skulls belong to are all still alive. Skin hangs from their faces, as thin as tissue and covered with age-spots. Sparks of cunning burn in the shadows of their empty eyes as they examine me.

"These are our masters," says my mother. "They call themselves the Dorians. The centuries pass and in the mirror they grow old but their bodies outside the mirror, in the world, stay young, full of life, powerful. The mirror is the secret of that power."

I stare.

"You've seen them now, O," says my mother. "You've seen our masters' true faces." She smiles and the smile makes me think of a shark. "Congratulations, my darling. You're a real Blank at last."

Chapter 12
The Fight

A moment passes.

"What happens now?" I ask her.

"We go to work," says M. "Together. You and me."

"What work?" I ask.

"The next mission," she says. "And the next. Wherever our masters need us, whatever they need."

I think about this some more, but I decided what I'm about to say long ago.

"No," I tell her.

M frowns, then takes a step towards me.

"Perhaps you don't understand what's happening here," she says. "Your mission tonight wasn't real." She tries another smile, to smooth over this difficulty.

"It was a test," she goes on. "Do you see? We let you think you chose to come here, but in fact tonight was the final test that all of us in the order must pass. We've been watching you all the way. Your every step has been studied, to assess your skills."

I blink.

"Oh, yes," she says. "We saw everything. I'll say this – the paraglider you used to get to the roof was a clever touch. But the rest, to tell you the truth, was fairly standard. We saw no real surprises – except, of course" – she nods past me – "out there in the corridor." She looks hard at me for a moment. "Let's be honest – you were sloppy. If I hadn't opened the door for you, the lasers would have cut you to pieces."

I feel my face start to flush, but I control it. I say nothing.

"Well, you've got a lot to learn," says M. "That's OK, I've got a lot to teach you. But first, darling, you've got to stop being a fool."

Maybe she's right. Maybe I am a fool. But it's a good ten years too late for her to do anything about that now. She is the last thing standing between me and what I came here to do.

I take a deep breath. Then I move my feet and put my fists up.

My mother stares at me in shock. "What do you think you're doing?"

"I'm going to fight you," I tell her.

"Why?"

"I'll tell you why if I win."

My mother raises an eyebrow. "I'd tell me now if I were you," she says. "I knew everything you know about fighting twenty years ago."

I take a deep breath and focus. I move forward to what I hope is the edge of M's reach.

"Let's find out," I say.

Then I go for her.

I start with two straight punches – a left jab low towards her body followed by a right jab to her face. My fists fly out then come back to a guard position, ready for anything. Or so I think.

M fends off my left fist but fails to block my right, which connects.

I've just punched my mother in the face.

M rocks back, her right hand at her nose. She gives me a look of horror.

"You *hit me*?" she says. Tears fill her eyes and her lip starts to wobble. "You'd do that? You'd hit your own mother?"

As I look at her, a sick taste of guilt wells up in the back of my throat.

"I'm sorry," I say. "I just ..."

I drop my arms and walk towards her – which, of course, is what she planned all along.

WHUD! She turns her hips and without even moving her right hand from her face she drives the point of her elbow into the side of my head. The blow lands just in front of my ear. My head fills with white noise, like a TV with no picture. But my mother is teaching me a lesson, and she hasn't finished yet.

A fist to my face rocks my head back on my neck, then I feel my mother's hands on my shoulders. She pulls me forward, steps in to meet me, and drives her right knee up into my stomach.

It's like a bomb going off inside me. My heels lift off the ground. My guts explode out of a hole in my spine – or that's how it feels.

My legs fold up. I drop to the floor and sit there like that, my head between my knees.

"Poor baby," says M, her voice sweet as she mocks me. "Did Mummy hurt you?"

I open my mouth but all that comes out is a stream of bile. Not the best answer.

"I don't understand you, O," says M. "Everything in your life has led up to this moment. Everything in your future depends on it. But here you are, in front of our masters, being sick on yourself." She stops in front of me. "Get up."

I feel like I've been shot with a cannon, but I follow her command without thinking. I'm standing before I know it.

M waves at the mirror full of grinning skulls.

"Bow," she says. "Tell our masters how sorry you are."

I lower my head. Then, before I have the chance to do something wise like change my mind ...

I charge.

The next few seconds seem to happen very slowly.

I'm running with my head down, like a bull.

I watch the floor pass beneath me as my feet take the steps – two, three, four.

M takes a neat step to one side, like a bullfighter. I'm going to end up going right past her. That's good. That's what I wanted to happen. Because I wasn't charging at her at all.

My hands snatch the Dorians' mirror out of the air.

Chapter 13
The Beginning

I've got it.

My guts are in agony. My knees are about to give out again. But I've done what I came to do. I grip the mirror in my hands and turn to face my mother.

Her mouth has fallen open.

"Let me check something with you," I say in a croak. I look down at the 66 Dorians, the rulers of the world. All they have for eyes are cold glints of light but, somehow, these have widened. I guess that means they're as surprised as M is.

"This mirror," I say, "is how the Dorians stayed alive all this time, is that correct? The part of them that's out in the world, their souls or whatever, are all connected to it. *The masters depend on the mirror.* Yes?"

"What are you thinking, O?" M asks, and I see her start to creep towards me. "What exactly are you trying to do here? Don't do anything rash, OK? At least until you've told me what you want."

That's when I'm sure. She's never asked me what I want before. No one has.

"I want to be free," I tell her.

I tighten my grip, and swing the mirror.

M tries to grab it, to stop me. She's far too late.

CRUNCH. The top left corner of the frame hits the wall beside me. The force of the blow spreads through the mirror.

For a long moment the magic inside the frame tries to hold on – instead of cracking like glass the mirror wobbles and bulges like a bubble. I see the jaws of the 66 skull faces of the Dorians open wide in 66 silent screams. Then the black wooden frame comes apart in my hands.

A pile of ash-grey crystals lands on the floor just in front of my feet. These melt, like slush, into a pool of wet which disappears almost at once with a puff of bad-smelling smoke.

There is a moment of stillness.

"Do you," M asks then, "have *any idea* what you've just done?"

I look at her. She seems to be looking at something I can't see.

"All over the world," she says. "Businessmen. Generals. Leaders. Kings. The 66 secret Rulers of the Earth, who have led us for more than 1,000 years … When the mirror broke they'll all have just … gone."

I'm very tired. Everything hurts.

"Yeah," I reply.

"But I've worked for the Dorians my whole life!" she says. She's babbling. "My parents worked for them, and my parents' parents, and my parents' parents' parents, and – "

I break in. "You don't work for them any more," I say. "Now no one does."

At last her eyes focus on me.

"But ... what will we do instead?" she asks.

"Whatever we want," I tell her.

Then I smile.

My name is O. Not zero, "O". Tonight, here, in the most secret room in the Bank of England, I have changed the world. I've freed myself. And I've freed *everybody else*.

There are no secret rulers of the world – not any more. There's no power that keeps people chained in lives that were planned for them before they were born. There's just us – me, you, everyone else, and whatever we want to do.

Right now the only person who knows this secret is you, as you read this.

It's a start.